Bible Stories

A GOLDEN BOOK®
Golden Books Publishing Company, Inc.
New York, New York 10106

We'd be happy to answer your questions and hear your comments. Please call us toll free at 1-888-READ-2-ME (1-888-732-3263). Hours: 8 AM–8 PM EST, weekdays. US and Canada only.

Joseph
and the Coat of Many Colors

Joseph's father loved Joseph so much that he gave him a present of a long, beautiful robe.

Joseph's brothers hated him for being their father's favorite, and were jealous of him.

Joseph said to his brothers, "I had a dream last night that we were tying bundles of straw and my bundle stood up. Then your bundles stood around mine, and bowed down!"

Joseph's brothers hated him all the more for his dreams.
His brothers would say, "Do you think that we would bow
down to YOU?"

One day, Jacob said to Joseph, "Go check on your
brothers tending the flocks, and bring me word."

"Here comes the dreamer!" said one of Joseph's brothers.

When Joseph arrived, his brothers took his beautiful coat.

Then they took him and threw him into a dry well.

Then they took him and threw him into a dry well.

"Let's sell Joseph as a slave to the Ishmaelites!"

Joseph's brothers sold him to the Ishmaelites
for twenty pieces of silver.

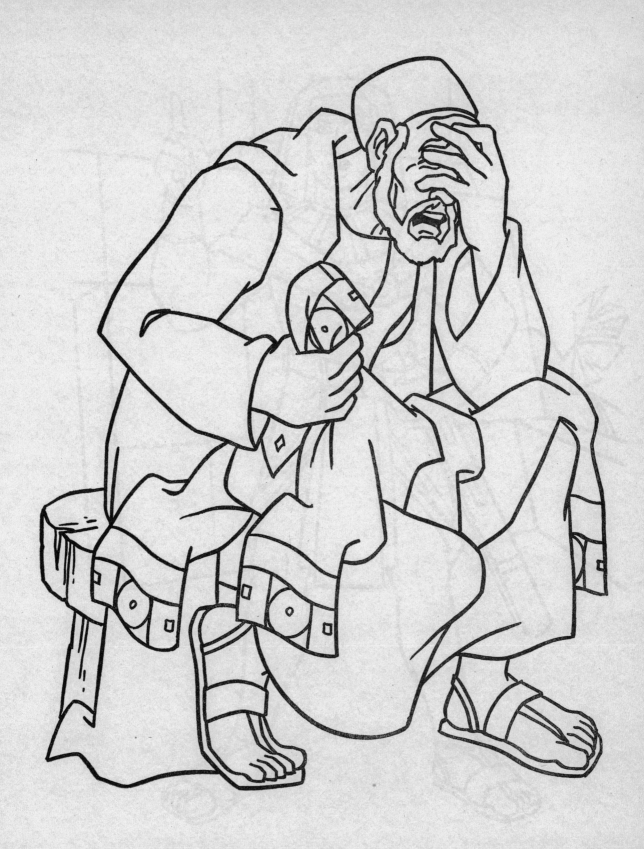

Joseph's brothers gave their father his coat,
and told him that he was killed by a wild animal.

Joseph was sold to Potiphar, an officer of Pharaoh.

Potiphar's wife did not like Joseph.
She told lies about him to get him in trouble.

Joseph was put in jail because of the things
Potiphar's wife said.

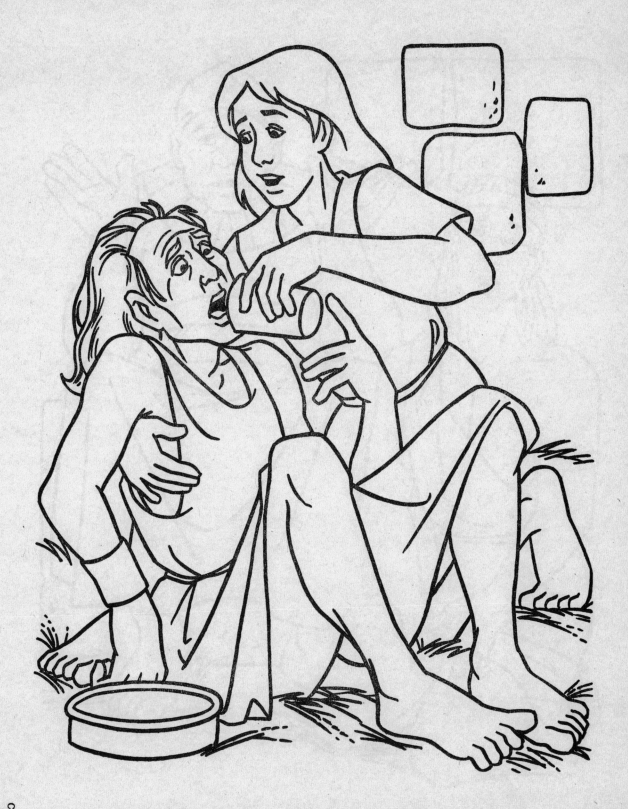

Joseph became well respected in the prison
and was in charge of the other prisoners.

The Pharaoh's butler and the Pharaoh's baker who had also been imprisoned each told Joseph of their troubling dreams.

Joseph told the butler what his dream meant.
He said, "Within three days Pharaoh will take you
out of prison and give you your job back."

Then Joseph told the baker the meaning of his dream.
The baker was frightened because his dream meant that
he would not be set free

Joseph's meanings were right. After three days
the butler was released.

The butler remembered Joseph when the Pharaoh was
having bad dreams. He told Pharaoh about Joseph,
and that Joseph would be able to tell him
what his dreams meant.

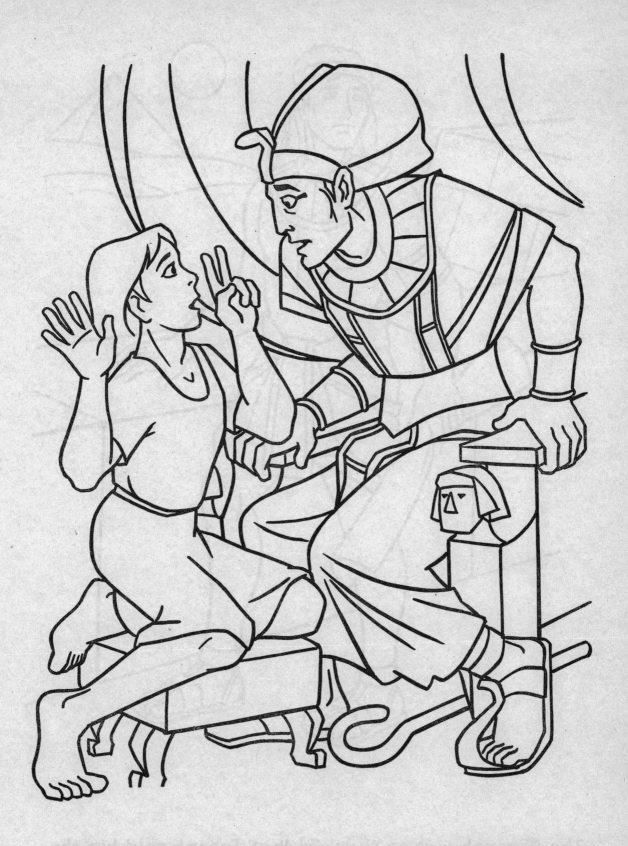

Joseph told the Pharaoh what his dreams meant.
He said, "There will be seven years of plentiful crops
followed by seven years of hunger and famine."

The Pharaoh was so thankful that Joseph told him the meaning of his dreams that he gave Joseph authority over all of Egypt to prepare for the seven years of hunger.

The seven years of bountiful harvest came.
Joseph had the grain stored away to prepare
for the seven years of famine.

Throughout the seven years of famine
there was food in Egypt, thanks to Joseph.

Joseph's brothers did not recognize him when they came to beg him to sell them food.

Joseph said to his brothers, "I am Joseph!
Is my father still alive?"

Jacob finally greeted Joseph, his son whom he thought was dead, and said, "I am so happy that I have seen your face, and know that you are still alive."

David and Goliath

David was a brave and caring shepherd.
He tended his father's sheep and was a good protector.

One day the Lord said to Samuel the Prophet, "Fill your horn with oil and I will send you to Jesse the Bethlehemite. One of his sons will replace Saul as king of Israel."

"This is the biggest and strongest of all of my sons.
He would surely please the Lord."

The Lord said to Samuel, "This man shall not be king!
I judge by what is in the heart and not by bodily strength."

"Surely the Lord will be pleased with one of
my younger sons!" said Jesse.

"My youngest son is tending the sheep.
I will send for him to come right away."

"David, you must come right away to your father's house.
The Prophet Samuel is there and he wants to see you!"

The Lord said to Samuel, "This is the one you will anoint."

Samuel took the horn of oil and anointed David in front of
his brothers, and the Spirit of the Lord came mightily upon
David from that day on.

King Saul who had always found favor in the sight of the Lord was no longer favored. David had taken Saul's place in the eyes of the Lord while an evil spirit began to torment King Saul.

One of Saul's advisors said, "Send your servant to find someone who plays the lyre, and when the evil spirit is upon you, he will play it, and you will feel better."

David was known to be a skillful lyre musician,
and was brought to serve King Saul. Saul was very
fond of him, and he even became Saul's armor-bearer.

At that time, the Philistines gathered their armies
for battle against Israel.

David's brothers fought the Philistines in battle. David found
his brothers on the battleground and he brought them food
from their father.

The Philistine's largest warrior, Goliath, challenged the
Israelites. "Choose a man to fight me. If he beats me, we
will be your servants; but if I win, you shall be our servants.
I defy the ranks of Israel this day!"

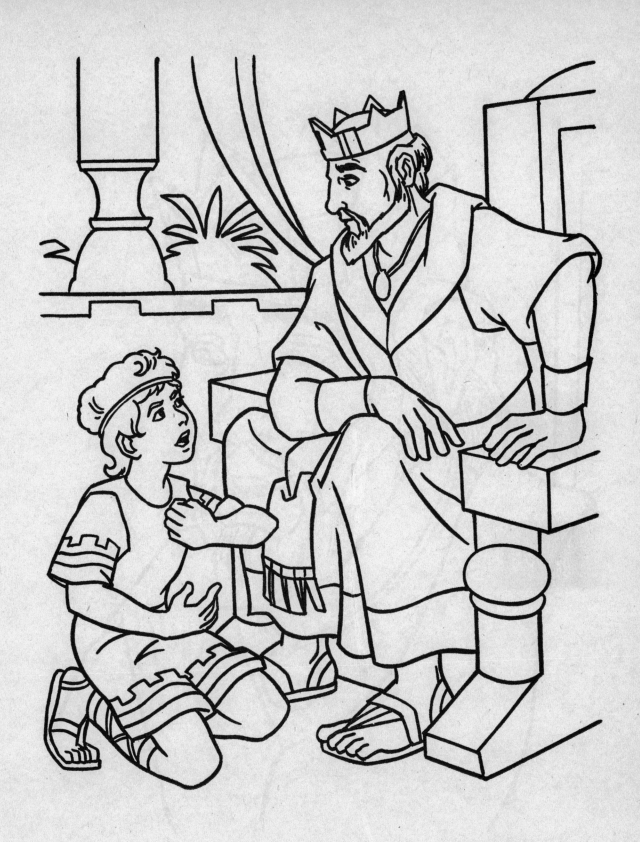

"Let no man's heart fail because of this Philistine;
I will go fight him."

"You are not able to go to fight against this Philistine. You are only a boy, and he has been a warrior from his youth."

"When a lion or bear took a lamb from my father's flock I went after it, killed it and delivered the lamb out of its mouth. I have killed both lion and bear; and this Philistine will be like one of them."

Saul agreed to let David fight Goliath, the Philistine.
He dressed David in the best armor.

I am not used to wearing armor and will not be able to fight with it on. David took off the armor and went to fight Goliath with no protection.

"Am I a dog, that you should come to me with sticks?
I will give your flesh to the birds of the air and the animals
of the field."

"You fight me with a sword, but I fight you in the name of the Lord, the God of Israel. This day the Lord will deliver you into my hand, and all the earth may know that there is a God in Israel."

David prevailed over the Philistine with a sling and with a stone, and struck down the Philistine and killed him.

When the Philistines saw that their mighty champion was dead, they ran away. The men of Israel rose with a shout and chased the Philistines. The Israelites were victorious.

David was praised for his heroic deeds
and eventually became king of Israel.

Noah was a just and righteous man. Noah walked with God.

God said to Noah, "I am very angry! People have turned mean and bad! I am going to bring an end to all living things on Earth!"

God instructed Noah how to build the ark: "Make yourself an ark of cypress wood. Divide the inside of the ark into rooms. You will cover it inside and out with pitch.

"For behold, I will bring a flood of waters upon the earth
to destroy everything under the heavens.

"You and your sons and your wife and your sons'
wives will enter the ark.

"But I will establish my covenant with you. You will bring two of every sort of living thing into the ark to keep them alive with you. They shall be male and female."

The animals went two-by-two into the ark,
just as God had commanded.

"Also take with you every sort of food that is eaten. You will store it up, and it will serve as food for you and the animals."

Then the Lord shut Noah and the animals in,
and closed the door around them.

It rained so much that the highest mountains were covered with water.

God remembered Noah, and the ark, and made a wind blow over the earth and the waters began to sink.

Noah sent a dove out to see if it could find dry land.
However, the dove couldn't find anywhere to rest.

After seven days, Noah sent the dove out again.
That evening it returned with an olive branch. Noah
now knew that the water was finally drying.

The ark came to rest on the mountains of Ararat.

All the animals left the ark by families.

Noah built an altar, and offered burnt offerings to the Lord.

God said to Noah, "Be fruitful, and multiply.
There will never be another flood to destroy the earth.

10/5/03

"This rainbow is a sign of my
promise to never flood the earth again."

After the flood, Noah lived 350 more years. He lived to be 950 years old. When you see a rainbow in the sky remember the story of Noah, and God's promise.